Mo and Ella Are Friends

D1502659

This is Mo.

Mo goes

Squeak squeak squeak!

Meet Mo and Ella

By Tui T. Sutherland
Illustrated by Rose Mary Berlin

For Kari—first friend, best friend. — TTS

Library of Congress Catalog Card Number: 00-107519

ISBN 0-448-42456-8   A B C D E F G H I J

Grosset & Dunlap • New York

This is Ella.
Ella goes
Clomp Clomp Clomp!

Ella has big feet
Can she go
Clomp Clomp Clomp!
now?
No!

Mo goes
Squeak squeak squeak!
Can Ella hear Mo?
No!

Now Mo goes
Squeak squeak squeak!

Oh!
Sorry, Mo!

It is hard for Ella to stop going
Clomp Clomp Clomp!

It is hard for Mo
to shout all the time.

How can they be friends?

Ella bends her trunk.
It goes
way, way down.

Mo goes up—
way, way up.

Ella puts Mo here.

Now Mo can go
Squeak squeak squeak!

Now Ella can go
Clomp Clomp Clomp!

Clomp Clomp Clomp!

Squeak squeak squeak!

Mo and Ella are best friends!

Mo and Ella at the Playground

Mo and Ella are best friends.

Let's go to the playground!

Off they go!
Clomp Clomp Clomp!

They try the swings.

Squeak squeak squeak!
This swing is too big!

But this swing is **too small!**

They try the slide.

Squeak squeak squeak!
This slide is too tall!

This slide is too skinny!

They try the seesaw.
Mo sits here.

Ella sits here.

Squeak squeak squeak!

Sorry, Mo.

Everything is too small
or too big.

This playground is for monkeys.

Let's go to the lake!

The lake is not too big.
The lake is not too small.

Squeak squeak squeak!

Clomp Clomp Clomp!

SPLASH!